CU01024886

Praise for Troy James Weaver & *Visions*

"Troy James Weaver's novel unravels the typical coming-of-age story. It erases the distinction between finding and losing your voice, becoming enlightened by a vision and swallowed by darkness. The plot moves at a breathless pace and the unsettling details linger, hovering at the edge of what can be fully understood."

—Jeff Jackson, author of *Mira Corpora*

"A noir fueled as much by the dread of what might happen as what actually occurs, with a narrator teetering on the edge of something very dark indeed. Beautifully sparse and precise, like someone tapping softly on your skull with a ball-peen hammer trying to feel out the perfect place to crack it open."

—Brian Evenson, author of *Windeye* and *A Collapse of Horses*

VISIONS

TROY JAMES WEAVER

VISIONS

Copyright © 2021 by Troy James Weaver

This is a work of fiction. Names, characters, businesses, places, events, locales, and incidents are either the products of the author's imagination or used in a fictitious manner. Any resemblance to actual persons, living or dead, or actual events is purely coincidental.

No part of this book may be reproduced in any form by any electronic or mechanical means including photocopying, recording, or information storage and retrieval without permission in writing from the author.

ISBN-13: 978-1-954899-99-5
ISBN-10: 1-954899-99-8

Cover design by Matthew Revert

Cover art by Eric Piper

www.apocalypse-party.com

Printed in the U.S.A

He was dangerous, irrational, and probably insane.
—President Bill Clinton

BEGINNINGS

That day, the first day, she didn't believe me, and it would be another three years before she finally would—and then only after she was dead.

I knew she'd be in the kitchen. She was always in the kitchen. She was cooking grits in a small pot, and had the radio turned up, listening to the old timey music she liked to listen to. I tugged on her arm to pull her away. She was thirty-three, still young, still pretty, and still willing to listen. I was only twelve years old when I told her about the voices and the lights that came to visit me at night.

She gathered her purse and keys and bus pass and told me to stay out of trouble while she was gone.

There was this lake I used to ride my bike to. It was only about a mile from our apartment, at the edge of town, and I liked to ride my bike out there and think long and hard about the world around me, the images and feelings which consumed me. Never learned much—just sort of sat there and wondered what it meant to be a boy with a dead dad.

I took my shoes off and dipped my feet into the water. I felt the minnows down there, darting around my toes.

I pulled my feet out of the water and dipped my hands in. I held them under a good long while and waited. Then I felt this chill run through me and clamped my fingers together. One small fish out of hundreds was now writhing in my hands. I threw him up on the bank and watched him flop. Then he was still. I looked skyward and picked him up and slowly lowered him back into the water. I massaged him a bit there until I felt some movement, and then I let him go.

I went back home and cleaned the grits from the pot. I shouldn't have let them sit so long. I wanted to pray and fall asleep on the spot. I wanted to be visited. I wanted the strange voice to come and tell me that there would be a day when the world would be delivered. And that would be the day when we'd actually be born.

And there was Joe. Joe was the second person I told about the angels and the voices and the light. I thought he believed me, too. He was a couple years older than me, and was the only other kid on the block. He told me once that he didn't care so much if his reputation was ruined for hanging out with me, and even though my feelings got hurt, in that moment I felt I needed him more than I ever had before.

I didn't know much about the bible and such and Joe told me he'd been to church a few times and would show me some things. He didn't mind, but he didn't want his mom finding out. She would give him a long hard whipping if she ever found out, he told me, so I went over there when she wasn't home.

When I got there he took me into his mom's bedroom. There was purple, paisley wallpaper on the walls. I told him I thought it was cool. *Thanks*, he said, *came with the place*, and as he said this he lowered his jeans and boxers to the floor. I started for the door, face flushed red, but he said, *No, don't go. This is it. This is what I wanted to tell you. You said you wanted to learn about god and the bible. Here it is: your first lesson. In the bible it says this is okay, in fact it's a duty.* I said, *Okay*, because I believed him. Then he told me to take him in my hand. I did. It was so small and hard in my hand it reminded me of the fish. Joe closed his eyes. He was breathing heavy, and within a minute or two he made a face like dying. When I wiped my hand on the carpet, Joe screamed, *Damn it, don't wipe it off on the floor*, and he stormed out of the room. He came back and wiped it up with toilet paper. On his knees he looked up and he said, *You can do it to yourself. It feels amazing. Some guy my mom knows taught me how to do it.*

The only other person I told that summer was a girl named Marilynn. She lived in the trailer park near the elementary school. I met her one afternoon after straying farther into town than usual. She was hopscotching, alone, across the street from the school, when I ran into her, the tree above her casting tiger-stripe shadows across her face. She was a cute girl, too, ten-and-a-half years old, with long hair down her back, all blonde and in a ponytail, and she seemed to cling to every word I spoke.

I told her everything—from the visions to the grits to the fish to my hand on the floor.

She listened and nodded, didn't offer words of advice or approval, didn't even smile. And it was nice, because it let me know she was really listening.

That's when I did it. I finally got up the courage to ask her something I'd wanted to ask somebody for as long as I can remember.

What's it like having a dad? I asked her.

She shrugged, let her eyes fall to the ground, and once again spoke in silence, kicking her foot into the sidewalk and tracing a circle into the dust with her toes.

Please, I said. *I need to know.*

Her eyes came up to connect with mine, and then she frowned. *You're not missing nothing.*

I couldn't stop thinking about all the awful things he must've done.

After that day, though, I stopped thinking about my own dad, because I finally realized that he'd always been there, with me, I just couldn't see him. I was my own dad and he was me, and we were one and not alone and never had been, not once, ever.

That night mom cooked up the other fish I caught. We ate it with white rice. We were always filling up on rice in those days—grits and rice, anything that'd stick to our ribs. We ate on a new tablecloth she'd brought home from work. I didn't notice it at first. And I tried to make it up to her by being overenthusiastic when I finally did.

Look at that blue! I said. *Where'd you get it?*

It's not blue, she said. *It's teal.* She smoothed out a small area of the cloth with her hands and told me she'd gotten it from a guy at work—told her he'd bought a new one for his wife and thought he'd bring the old one to his favorite waitress. When she was telling me about it, she kept fidgeting with her hands beneath the table. I wondered what he looked like. I could tell she liked him. I wanted to ask her if she liked him, if she thought he was father-material, but didn't.

I cut into the fish and took a bite, swallowed it down with some water.

Must be a nice man, I said.

Mom didn't say anything. I watched her for a minute. It was weird. It was as though she'd lost herself inside that strange color, moving her hands in small circles over the table.

From a notebook

A lot of lights, big flood-type lights fixed to four corners of the room, all white walls, and a block of wood the size of a coffin. I'm lain out over the block. I look to my left, then to my right. There are thousands of fish crudely drawn on plywood walls, lots of colors, lots of blacks and whites. A voice commands me still. I look straight above me. On the ceiling there's a mirror duct-taped against the popcorn-white. The voice, it's soft and high-pitched at the same time. It tells me to look at the mirror until I come to know myself. It tells me to practice with my thing in my hand. It tells me I'm dirty and alone and never going to be anything beyond the face in the mirror, the kid with the little bike and the hidden secrets. It says I need to learn to love the face in the mirror, even if the face in the mirror is unlovable. I tug on myself and smile into the mirror of myself, mouth the words "thank you" so many times my mouth starts to fill with blood.

The week before school started I saw Joe up in a tree with a girl. She looked a little older than him, wearing ripped jeans and a huge black t-shirt. She had a ton make up all over her face. She looked like she was dead, but wasn't, and I felt happy for Joe, because this strange dead girl had the power to make him smile a smile I didn't know he had. She was smoking a really long, skinny cigarette. She'd take a couple puffs then hand it to Joe. He choked every time he took a drag. Every time he choked, she laughed. I watched them, wondering if Joe had taught her about the Bible yet, or if that was something he did special just for me.

Finally, I approached them.

How's it going, Joe?

They ignored me, continued talking to each other, passing the cigarette between them.

Hey, I said, *how've you been*?

The girl finally looked down at me, glanced at Joe, and said, *You know this kid?*

Joe looked at me a minute, then said, *Yeah, I know him.*

He looked at the girl, then back down at me. *What's your name again?*

The dead-looking girl giggled.

Visions

No, seriously, I forgot. What is it?
We never talked to each other again, not while he was living.

Seventh grade was a lot different than sixth. I felt like I knew a whole lot more about the world, yet I didn't know what it was. I felt changed, different from the kid I was the year before, yet exactly the same.

Joe was in high school now, so I didn't see him much, but Marilynn was everywhere and all at once, and I couldn't get enough of her. I'd follow her around, tease her, flirt with her, watch her when she wasn't even looking, and after a few weeks, we even started walking home from school together.

There was the tree with Joe and the dead-looking girl we passed by on the way home from school. Sometimes they'd be up there, smoking cigarettes. Sometimes they wouldn't. Usually we just walked past them. Sometimes I'd look up at Joe and think of what I'd say if I were to say something. All I could ever come up with was: *I hope she's worth it,* but I knew how pathetic that sounded. Sometimes I looked at the dead-looking girl and wondered if Joe secretly wished she was me.

Marilynn hardly talked at all. When she did, it was real quiet. I had to take special pains to pay attention to her.

This, she said, holding out her hand, voice like a leaf blown over the pavement. *Take it. I want you to have it.*

I reached down and pulled the chain out of her palm. It was a gold chain, a necklace without clasps or pendants, about two feet long. I squeezed it into my fist and shoved my fist into my pocket, keeping it there.

Thanks, I said. *Why'd you give it to me?*

Can't tell you that, she said, blushing. *It means a lot, though.*

I took the gold chain home with me and hid it in the bathroom under the sink, because I didn't want mom wondering where I'd gotten it from—because the bathroom was the only place in the apartment where I felt I could keep my secrets hidden.

At the lake, Marilynn and I sprawled inches apart on the tall grass. The smell of fish and water, a cloud over us, the silence and stillness, and I kissed her on the mouth and asked if she'd like to learn about the bible someday.

Not really, she said. *Why?*

I shook my head and said, *I don't know. I was just wondering.*

I tried again a couple weeks later.

Want to learn about the bible?

Why you keep asking me that?

Just something to think about, I said. *Give it some thought.*

I was walking out of the school one day, looking for Marilynn, when I saw all these people out near the flagpole. They were all dressed up in nice suits and skirts and they were handing out small green books to all the kids. I ran up and got one for myself. I made it halfway out of the parking lot before I even realized what it was. It was a bible, the real deal, all bound in green vinyl with gold lettering that peeled away at even the slightest touch.

I ran home as quickly as I could.

I read it in the bathroom with Marilynn's gold chain draped around my neck. I read it for three hours straight. Mom thought I was sick or something, staying in the bathroom so long. I tried to tell her I was all right, but she just kept saying, *No, no. You're sick, son. You need to go get into bed.*

I stayed home the whole week. In the mornings, mom would come in and slip a thermometer under my tongue. She'd stand there staring at the perfectly healthy temperature, waving the thermometer back and forth, saying, *There's something wrong with it. Says your fine, but look at you—you're sweating.*

From a notebook

A voice comes to me in total dark. It's not just one voice. Seems like a thousand different voices. They're all saying the same thing. They're saying, One and one and one and one and one and one and one and one and one and one and one and one and one and one and one and one and one. My throat starts to tighten, squeezes the breath out of me, the longer they go on like that. My bedroom door opens up and a hard wall of light pours in. Smells like burnt wood and something else. Coca-Cola and bologna sandwiches, all the things I was ever taught at school.

The next week, back at school, Marilynn was mad at me, said she'd waited and waited for me outside the school that day.

But you never came, she said. *Where were you?*

I told her I was sick.

Yeah, she said. *Sick with what?*

Fever, I said.

Marilynn didn't say anything but sort of gave me a sideways grin.

I'm sorry, I said. *Forgive me?*

She took my hand, silently, and walked me toward the tree where Joe and his dead-looking girlfriend were perched.

She said, *Look at them.*

I looked at them. Joe was blowing smoke out of his nose, arms clasped around the dead-looking girl's waist, and she was fooling with this red pocket knife, cutting into the bark from time to time. Joe's clothes looked different, his style. He was wearing rips in his jeans and a dirty white t-shirt. His hair was greased back. The girl looked just the same as always, only paler, and on the upper places of her arms, near the nooks, bruises stuck out in clusters.

Is that us? she said.

No, I said. *I don't think so.*

Marilynn looked deep into me, an uncomfortable stare, squeezing my fingers even tighter in her soft little hand.

In a way, I said, *I guess it is—I don't know.*

At night, in the bathroom, when I was supposed to be bathing, I took to tugging on myself like I'd tugged on Joe. In fact, the first time I did it, I pictured him doing it, teaching me, but after a while, maybe two weeks later, Joe's face and hands slowly became Marilynn's face and hands. We all became one. I wrapped the gold chain she'd given me around it when I did it. It was better that way. But, usually, after several minutes of tugging, I'd tire and start for the bible I kept in a plastic bag in the tank of the john. I'd pull it out, set it on the sink, and pee with my thing stiff and sticking straight up so that I'd have to bend almost ninety-degrees to get it out of me and into the pot. Then I'd plop down on the john and read all the old timey words I didn't understand but liked the sound of.

A few weeks after I started doing this, Marilynn told me the story behind the gold chain, why she wanted me to have it—why it ever meant so much to her in the first place.

Momma gave it to me the morning the tractor trailer slammed into her on I-40, she said, words deadpan, like she'd been shocked out of her old voice and fitted with a new one. *I told her not to go. I had a bad feeling inside me. Like I'd seen it all, knew what was gonna happen, but I just didn't trust the details or something.*

I looked at my right shoe. The sole was flapping off, showing a dirty sock. I looked at my other shoe. It looked great, compared. I looked at a stick which lay in the dirt near a bush not five feet in front of us. I thought it looked like a bull snake before I thought it looked like a stick. And before that, I thought it looked a bit like a tiny bolt of lightning. Course it wasn't any of those things. It was just a piece of old rebar, all bent up and rusted to hell. I thought of all the great things rebar must be used for, though I didn't even know what rebar really was or what it was used for. I'd just heard Joe say it one time while swinging a metal rod. I heard him say it again. *You could kill someone with a piece of this here rebar,* his voice and words like long shadows in my head.

I felt a tug at my arm.

You listening to me?

Yeah, I'm listening. I heard you. You said you knew it was going to happen, like you'd seen it all before—you just didn't want to believe it.

Yes, she said. *But it wasn't like you. It wasn't a vision or anything like that. It was just a sick feeling in my stomach. It was a feeling like I was going to puke or something.*

You know they've left me, don't you, I said. *Haven't had one in three months. Can't even get them to come if I try.*

But I was lying. I just wanted her to feel special.

From a notebook

They will tell you you're nothing special, it says. You are special. You are more special than they.

One day my teacher said something to me. She pulled me off into the corner of the room after school and said, *You having problems at home?*

No ma'am.

Grades are slipping, she said.

I looked down to the ground.

What's going on? You started off on the right foot.

I kept my eyes on the ground, shook my head. *I don't know. Just having troubles concentrating, that's all.*

We stood there in silence for a few minutes.

That girl you been running around with, she said. *I've seen you two out around town together. That girl's got more problems than a one-armed—*

It's not her fault, I said. *I told you. I'm just having trouble concentrating, that's all.*

Well, all right, she said. *Just try getting your head back in the game.*

At the edge of the lake I could see a bunch of fish all bellied-up. Bloated and floating in clusters. They looked like constellations jam-packed with sick stars. I didn't fish that day or the next, not in the traditional sense, and it made me feel bad, because mom was always hungry. You could hear it in her voice at night.

Just a few days after I discovered the dead fish, Marilynn touched me for the first time, and afterward, we walked across the baseball diamond to Walt's Diner to try to get some free ice cream from mom. While mom was trying to sneak us some vanilla, Old Man Stafford, who always smelled like rubbing alcohol, told me what it was that killed those fish. The soap factory had dumped something awful into the lake. He forgot what it was called, but he sure knew it was bad. I asked him why he thought they did it, but he wouldn't tell me. He just sort of grunted, sipped his coffee, and said, *Cheap sons-of-bitches*. I didn't really understand what he meant by it, but I knew he didn't like them. I couldn't stop from wondering about it. If I got into the lake, would the bad stuff kill me, like it had the fish, or would it make me feel the fish-feel of being out of water then coming back to life?

It happened at the park near the bushes by the tennis courts. It was quiet, deserted, about to rain. All the kids making way home for their afterschool work and dinner. But there was something else in the air, too. Something I couldn't figure right. We were sitting there, Mare and I, just talking to each other—not talking about anything, really, just talking. Then she grabbed my leg out of nowhere, clenched up close to the groin, and pulled my face close. She hesitated a moment, then she kissed me. It was lightning-quick, her head pulling back with this wild look all through her.

Teach me that thing Joe taught you, she said.

From a notebook

Trees and buildings and dust and a hundred people gathered around me. I'm older. Glasses thick and ugly on my face, I have long hair and cutoff jean shorts. The sun is burning away the water in a trough. It's sucking it right up before our eyes. I'm chanting and ranting and raving. I look like a very happy man with sad and failing eyes. People cheer. I don't even know what I'm saying, I'm just saying it, and everything seems cool and natural and wonderful, except for the piercing sirens which nobody seems to notice but me—an awful wailing all filled with light and heat and something completely beyond any one of us of earth.

Halfway through the school year, Joe and the dead-looking girl ran away together. Took off for Biloxi, what I heard. They hadn't been in the tree in a couple weeks, so I asked this kid named Frank who was in Joe's class. *Took off,* he said. *Stole a car and took off for Biloxi. They been getting all hopped-up on drugs and having sex all the time—kept getting caught. I think they're in love.*

Marilynn and I were getting in some serious fool-around time at the park, just as I imagined Joe was in his stolen car all over Biloxi—and I still wasn't doing so well in school on account of my mind not being there, not even in the retard class, which is what the man mom brought home for dinner called it. *Your momma tells me they got you in the retard class. Why's that? You're a smart boy, anyone can see that.*

I cheated, I told him.

The man mom brought home for dinner was named Ray. He was a baldy with a huge mustache and sacks under his eyes. He smelled like a country ham mixed in with the wash, cigarette smoke and tooth paste. Sweat poured down his face eighty percent of the times I saw him. Sometimes I'd wake up and find him there in the morning, eating bacon and eggs and drinking orange juice from the carton, and I'd think: Well, at least we're eating better.

This was the scene that saw me into my first year of high school, into mom's death—Marilynn, mom, and Ray all mainstays, even though I never acknowledged Ray as much more than a prop in my life, a stand-in father, and even though the cancer would eventually make mom merely a ghost inside me.

It was clear this time. I saw it all play out like a TV show—Joe and his dead-looking girlfriend, their car wrapped around a tree, their teenaged bodies bent in reverse, broken, and their small little mouths slopped open like dead-hog lips, dribbling blood in streams all over the back seat, where they'd been pushed back and pinned beneath the steel.

The voice I heard was Joe's voice, though his lips didn't move. He was saying my name over and over, a bit muffled and blood-gargled. I reached out to him, to his voice, but it all faded away, just like that, when the sound of mom and Ray doing sexy things in the other room unexpectedly snaked through the walls.

I listened carefully to what they were doing, especially to mom. She seemed to enjoy it.

At least he's making her feel good, I thought.

Marilynn and I passed by the Post Office a few weeks later and saw my vision right there on the front page of our small town paper: RUNAWAY TEENS IN FATAL CAR WRECK.

That night, we met up by the tree around midnight and carved our names into the trunk up near where Joe and his girlfriend used to sit and smoke cigarettes. Then we cut the tips of our pointer fingers and pressed them together. I could hear the sound of our blood mixing. The sound was lush, a bubbling, like soap suds popping, and it gave me an erection. The gold chain was down there, cutting into me. I wanted to kiss her, but felt like it would be a dishonor to the dead, so instead I took the lesser or routes and just held her bloody hand. She was acting strange, though, like she was embarrassed or something, and eventually she pulled her hand free from mine to dig a cigarette from her pocket. It took four turns on the lighter to get it going.

What're you doing? I said.

Smoking, she said.

You smoke? I said.

I do now, she said.

So I smoked it with her, coughing every time I took a drag, and wishing, with every pull, I could take away all the illness in the world and fit it inside me.

When I crawled through the window, sneaking back into the apartment, an invisible force grabbed me by the shirt collar and slammed me against the wall.

Where the fuck've you been? Your mother's been worried sick.

I couldn't see anything, but I knew his voice and the smell of his skin—I knew his anger. It was Ray, and he'd only been getting meaner since news of the lumps in mom's boobs started eating its way through his head.

Answer me, he said.

I went to the lake.

What're you doing at the lake in the middle of the night? He said.

Couldn't sleep, I said. *I took a walk and ended up at the lake.*

Couldn't sleep?

I shook my head.

How come you couldn't sleep? he said.

I could hear you two doing whatever it is you were doing, I said.

He didn't say anything for a minute, just shook his head.

Go on, get in bed, you little pervert, he said.

Marilynn had an uncle, Jessup, who talked nearly as much as Ray did, only he was poorer, and instead of bacon, he smelled like road kill and hairspray. Jessup was twenty-five, pale, skinny, tall, with this dark brown hair short all over except a thin long strip that hung down his back like a dirty shredded ribbon.

Met him walking out of school with Marilynn one day—said we looked cute together then offered a ride in his grey F-150.

More than once we took him up on his offer.

He listened to loud music with a lot of screeching and screaming. He told me about how cool his place was, said I should stop by sometime to check it out. He told me he had all kinds of board games, always had soda in the fridge—he even had a TV.

In front of my apartment, he scribbled his address on a piece of scratch paper and handed it to me. I shoved it into my pocket and hopped out of his truck. I was so excited about the prospect of seeing his place I told him *I'll see you tomorrow* and ran inside instead of taking off on my bike like I usually did.

Mom wasn't home yet, working still, even with the lumps and the treatments, and Ray was mad at the President again—mad at the "whole goddamn, sonofabitch of a situation we're in over there," meaning the war.

You hear me, fucker?

I nodded and listened to him rave, didn't dare say anything because I didn't want mom to ever have to feel the awful weight of loneliness again. She was happy with Ray. And he never did any of the bad things he did to me when she was home or awake or when I was locked away in the bathroom, reading away my sins.

One day I bagged up a few of the dead floaters at the lake and brought them home. Didn't look so dead as not to eat, not yet, and since I'd grown lazy with their watery, weedy flavor, there was this hunger inside me, not of the gut, really, but the mind.

But as soon as I brought them into the kitchen Ray got all mad at me and made me throw them in the trash.

Don't bring them stinky sonsofbitches in here, he said. *I fucking hate fish—they're filthy little things.*

I didn't even catch these on a pole, I said. *These were just floating up top on the water like that.*

I don't give a shit, he said.

Fine, I said. *Just like you, I understand not liking things.*

From a notebook

I awake in a field. A field with rusted old cars piled around me. I see mom in front of one of the cars, cooking eggs on an overheated radiator. She's scrambling them. There is a man in the front seat of the car, driver side, sleeping with his head flung out the window. High-pitched voices fill me. Singing. Words I can hear. Words I understand. They're hidden in these bright lights. They're saying, You and you and you will be you're salvation. Mankind, that's you. And beneath this voice a current like water takes me to a place on a hill in a canoe to see a few good men being nailed to crosses. And Ray is among them.

I rode my bike to Jessup's apartment one Saturday. It was a four mile bike ride. When I got there, I was covered with sweat and sun-reddened in the face. My skin hurt, legs all jelly and bone-sore, hips begging to pop out of joint and fall away.

I knocked on the door, and was inside within seconds, sipping a soda and admiring the walls.

Jessup had these posters all over with long-haired guys on them, wearing leather and plaid and rips in their jeans—all musical bands I'd never head of—AC/DC, Megadeth, Suicidal Tendencies—and the TV was on, volume turned way up, showing horrific scenes of bloodied bodies and lipstick-written messages on white walls. The room was filled with smoke. He had a soda in his hand, silver can, and was talking out loud to himself about the show he was watching. It reminded me of the way Ray ranted on and on about his politics.

Richard fucking Ramirez was the best there ever was, he said. *Dude had it all—good looks, an incredible personality, great hair—evil to the fucking gills—plus he loved AC/DC!*

I nodded, uncomfortably, and swigged some soda.

I didn't know who he was talking about but was pretty sure it had something to do with all the carnage on the TV—the foreign-looking guy with the long brown hair who had his hand up in the courtroom, showing off a drawing of an upside-down star with a circle around it.

Jessup said, *Hold on a minute,* and left the room.

When he came back, he threw me a towel. I spoke through it as I wiped the sweat off my face. *Who is he?*

What?

I pulled the towel down, set it on my lap. *I said 'who is he?'*

Serial killer, he said. *Best there ever was, too—well, I don't know, maybe not the best, but definitely one of my all-time favorites.*

I kept wondering why he liked this Richard guy so much, this killer of women of all ages, shapes, and sizes.

Him? I said, pointing at the TV. *What's so great about him?*

What's so great about him, he said. *Just look at him. He's fucking awesome.*

We sat there silent a moment. Then I told him I'd been reading the bible and that I didn't think it was a good thing to *like* killers of women—or even killers of men—killers of anybody.

Then there was another space of silence, the kind of silence that filters through the TV and radio noise, even the sound of the yelling neighbors.

Then I told him in the bible it said hell was filled with people like this Richard guy.

And you believe that shit? he said.

All the noise rushed back in—the neighbors, the TV, the radio.

I nodded that I believed it, but I wasn't really sure.

What else is there? I said.

Lots of things, he said. *You're just too young to get the picture.*

What picture?

Visions

I'll take you out some night, he said. *You'll get the picture*
I felt uncomfortable so I asked where the bathroom was.
That door, right there, he said, pointing through a hallway.
Midstream, he knocked on the door.

If you like tits, the mags are under the sink. I fingered the chain
as I peed. *Just don't get them sticky,* he said.

There was a green ring from the chain. I wore it down there most every day. Marilynn was curious what all the green was about. I couldn't tell her that. I couldn't tell her that her dead mother's chain was a constant source of pleasure—that it reminded me of Joe—and that everything seemed to slip away whenever the chain tightened, cutting into my skin, and when it did, all I could think about was what it might be like to die side by side by side with the people I love.

There was one tiny movie theatre in town. Mare and I snuck in one night and watched one of the pictures. It was an old one, had a guy with a deep voice playing at being a cowboy, looking for a kidnapped girl. The Indians had taken her. It seemed to get the crowd all kinds of excited. I thought it was okay. I especially liked one of the little Indian girls—looked like Mare, with darker skin and lighter eyes. I just kept hearing this voice that said, *Teach her, teach her, teach her—teach her about the bible, tell her about our ways.*

I met up with Jessup in the cemetery in the middle of the night. He was wearing a really long black coat, black lipstick on his cold pale lips. He looked like one of the guys in one of the posters he had tacked to his walls. He put small white candles on top of some tombstones and lit them. It was a windless night, cold enough to see your breath. He spread a quilt over the grass. We sat down, shivering, pulling our coats up around our necks. Then he set this brown and tan board between us. It was a strange looking board, filled with letters and numbers, a moon, a sun, the words YES, NO, HELLO, and GOODBYE. He put a piece of plastic that looked like an upside-down heart with glass in the center of it on the board—he called it a Wee-Gee board, but he must've been pronouncing it wrong, because at the top of the board, what it said was Ouija.

My cuz tells me your dad's dead, he said.

I nodded.

So's Mare's mom, you know?

I nodded again, clenching my teeth against the cold.

Fall leaves were scattered around us. You could hear them, scratchy in their piles, even over the highway traffic which came through a half-mile distance.

Jessup adjusted himself and lit a cigarette. *Okay,* he said, *first thing's first—what's your dad's name?*

What *is* my dad's name?

I shrugged. *I don't know,* I said. *I've never even thought about it before.*

Jessup didn't say anything, really, just made a noise: uhhhh.

I looked at him. He looked uncomfortable.

I'm sorry, he said. *I didn't really think about that being an issue.*

I tried to assure him that it wasn't an issue, that I wasn't really sad about it. I'd never known him, ever, which I imagine is less painful than losing somebody when you are still alive enough to remember. I wasn't even born yet when he died, is what my mom told me, so the only pain I could possibly feel was the pain of not knowing what was lost.

I told Jessup to go on, leave it alone, and get on with the board game.

Whole fucking game is ruined, he said. *That's the thing. We can't contact your dad without his name. That would be fucking impossible, man.*

Well, I said, *what about Marilynn's mom. You know her name, don't you?*

Jessup got really quiet and his shoulders slunk down. *No,* he said.

You don't know her name?

Of course I know her fucking name—she's my oldest of three sisters, he said, blowing smoke through his nostrils, *but I'm not going to do that.*

He ditched the cigarette and dug his fists into his eyes, like he was crying, but ripped them away after only a few seconds, yawned, and said he was getting tired.

Let's just do this one, here, he said.

What?

That one, there, he said, pointing his finger at a tombstone.

It was really dark, even with the candles, so I had a hard time trying to make out what was written on the stone.

Jessup stood up and walked over to the tombstone, squinting. *Robert Childress Hackinsaw,* he said. *That's the one.*

He came back over and sat across from me. He told me how to put my fingers on the upside-down heart piece. Then he put his fingers on the other side. He placed a candle on the board so we could read the letters.

Wee-gee, we are here for Robert Childress Hackinsaw, he said. *Robert, we come in peace and mean no ill toward you. We just want to ask you a few questions. Is that okay, Robert?*

I could feel Jessup pushing the piece with his fingers. I tried to resist his pull, but he just kept going. His face was getting red. I knew what he wanted. He wanted contact. I let the piece ease across the board to the YES, just as he wished, because I wanted him to believe just as much as I did.

Robert, he said, eyes closed, facing the sky, *was your death accidental, plotted, or did you die of natural causes?*

I let the piece move about the board.

It spelled out S-U-I-C-I-D-E.

I asked him what it meant.

He looked at me as though I were the kid that skipped a few letters and replaced them with slurred grunts and hums while singing the ABCs in a room full of geniuses.

It's when somebody kills themselves, he said.

Visions

He explained all the different methods.

Scary shit, he said.

I wondered if my dad had suicided or if he'd just died like a normal person dies.

Fuck this, he said. *Let's get out of here. Suiciders are the ones you really don't want to fuck with.*

When I went to blow out one of the candles, I saw the dates on the tombstone:

Robert Childress Hackinsaw

September 13th, 1978—July 7th, 1979

That was the first of two signs Jessup would betray me. He just had this silly air of the magician about him. Did he really expect me to believe that a baby had hung itself or shot itself or cut its tiny little wrists? And then there's the other thing. The night I went over there and caught him giving alcohol to Marilynn. She was already feeling funny when I got there, looked to be pretty much gone to it. He told me it was okay, Jesus drank wine, made gallons of it with his magical superpowers. And then I let him convince me to drink some, too. Marilynn told me it was fun. *Don't be such a wet blanket,* she said. So I said, *Shoot, give me one of those.* I drank about six cans of the stuff. I couldn't move, couldn't get myself up from the beanbag chair. There was this song playing on the radio with some guy that kept screeching *hells bells.* I kept drifting in and out of sleep. And it was in that sleep that I saw Jessup remove Marilynn's shirt and touch her little breasts. I saw a man on the TV stabbing a woman in the shower. I saw Jessup take Marilynn's hand and wrap her tiny fingers around his penis. I saw a poster that said *DIO.* I saw Jessup put his penis in Mare's mouth, clenching a fistful of her hair. I saw a coffee table filled with at least thirty empty beer cans and thousands of cigarette butts. I saw Jessup moving around a lot, hovering over Marilynn, grunting. Above me, I saw brilliant yellow stains on the ceiling. I saw Jessup slump to the floor, pants still around his knees, closing his eyes. I saw the center of his chest, quivering like a wounded animal. There was a noise next door, somebody yelling. Suddenly, Jessup was snoring. I saw the last game of Risk we'd played the week before, on the table near the kitchen, and then I saw Marilynn. She was still lying on the couch, all alone—she was so alone. Her eyes were closed, her breathing shallow. I could feel the alcohol losing its hold on me, but my mind was a scream of a thousand different colors, all at once, and I was lost somewhere between sleep and vision.

THE MOVEMENT OF THINGS

From a notebook

Left of me is a face without a face, just skin stretched over bone, a cross scarred across it sideways, no eyes, no mouth, just the scar, and to the right of me, a face with multiple faces, like the eyes of a fly, a bunch of faces on this side, a bunch over here, they're everywhere but crammed together in one space that's the size of a regular face. Some have beards, some are clean shaven, some are women, and some are children. All of them are chanting. They keep saying, all of them, Love thy self, Love thy treasons, Love thy self, Love thy lullabies, Love thy self, Love thy suicide, Love thy self, Love thy treasons, Love thy self, Love thy lullabies, Love thy self, Love thy suicide, Love thy self, Love thy life, Love thy death, Love thy suicide...

It wasn't long before mom quit working. The treatments made her feel worse than anything—depleted her body and soul—and so she took to bed most days, straight through the night.

Ray splurged and bought a TV, which was placed atop the dresser under a picture of Elvis.

He eventually moved in with us, instead of vice versa, due to mom's stubbornness in wanting to stay put, even though we could've used a bigger place. Sure, from the bible I'd learned of its wrongness, being unwed and living together, but honestly, I couldn't find any harm in it, because it really made her happy, us all being together.

When the drought hit, freshman year, the lake dried up so that you could walk straight across it and never even come close to touching water. I wanted to mourn its passing, but hadn't even fished it in almost two years, not with a pole, so I saw this emptiness, this big dry hole, as the perfect place to come out to and paint my life upon.

I was at the lake the day the chain finally broke off my bike. I was too big for it and I was pedaling up some tough terrain. Snapped off like it was millions of years old—nothing but a piece of dust holding it together. I'd been out there playing with myself, thinking of all the fish that died—specifically the fish I killed and brought back to life. Then I started thinking of Joe. I missed him. I saw his face, the same face I saw that day in his mom's bedroom. Then I felt a whole bunch of lightning shoot through me, all these pins and needles, my butthole tightened into a knot, and my hand was suddenly filled with sticky life. There were spurts of the stuff on the rocks I was standing on. Momentarily, I was blinded. And that's when I realized that everything I'd been taught had in some way been truth—even those weird words in the bible. I hardly understood it, any of it, but I was getting closer and closer, with each and every passing day, to getting a foothold.

When the visions started more frequently, it was spring, another year gone, and mom had stopped keeping house, completely. For a little while, even after she'd quit her job, she at least still got up to dust and sweep the floor, though she only did so in quick spurts and with little to no energy. With mom no longer cleaning, Ray would come home angry and yell at her. Not always, but on nights when he came home late from the bar, this was the truest of truths our air could offer. I'd tell him I'd clean up the place. I'd tell him it was my fault the place was such a mess, to leave mom alone, that I'd clean it all up, but he'd slap me and yell at me to go to my bedroom. I could hear it all through the walls, him yelling at my poor, sick mother.

That kid wants to do fucking woman work!

What the hell kind of kid are you raising!

You want him to be a fucking fairy when he grows up! The kind of guy who takes his dick out and waves it at strangers at bus stops!

There was one window in the living room. After Ray got fired from the Waterworks, he hung mom's teal tablecloth over it to block out the sunlight. The light made his head hurt worse than the alcohol he'd started drinking—maybe even worse than the belt he'd begun swinging across my shins. He always sounded like he was dying, groaning and bellowing and cursing. After the tablecloth went up over the window, nothing really changed—the room just grew darker.

All the sudden I was fourteen years old, officially dating Marilynn now that the door-to-door magazine job I'd landed finally afforded me a date here and there. Still, I only ever brought her into the apartment two times in those days. Even though I knew it would end badly, even though I'd seen it all play out in my dreams, my whole entire life, I wanted mom to meet her before she died—I even wanted Mare to say 'hello' to Ray—to maybe even sit down and stay awhile, eat some of that famous bacon Ray fried up and listen to a few old timey songs with mom on the radio in the kitchen.

There was a knock at the door at 6:30: Marilynn. I gave her the smallest little kiss on her cheek and yelled out that our company had arrived. Mom struggled into the kitchen with her walker, all rickety and looking ancient. Ray was already in there, sipping back on some whiskey in a puddle of sweat. The radio was blurting out some old crooner tune—Mister Lonely by Bobby Vinton.

Mom laid one eye on Marilynn's long sun-blonde hair, her smooth, reddened skin, and perfect round face and she burst into tears. Bacon was spitting in the frying pan, Ray just letting it do its thing, while he sat there with his drink, looking unhealthy in his bathrobe.

Hey, there, hush yourself in front of guests, Ray said. *That or go into the other room, for god's sake.*

I gave him the hard stare. Marilynn didn't know what to do. Mom just kept staring at Marilynn and crying these tears. She'd never cried like that before, ever.

Well, Ray said, *if you aren't gonna go, I will. Just watch the fucking bacon. That's all we need, you burning the place down.*

He went into their bedroom and slammed the door.

Mom smiled, took Marilynn's hand in hers, and asked me to leave them alone for a few minutes, her voice all weak and whispery.

I didn't really understand what was going on, but I excused myself from the table and went into the bathroom.

I did all the old familiar things. Gold chain around my penis, I tugged and tugged and tugged. I sat down on the john, wiped the sweat from my face and tried to listen to what they were talking about through the door.

All I could hear was the radio.

I pulled the bible from the tank and read from it at random.

It wasn't the first or second or even third thing I read—it was the sixth, and where my finger landed, this is what it said:

And if any mischief follow, then thou shalt give life for life...

I put the bible back in the tank of the toilet and went back into the kitchen.

Mom still had Marilynn's hand in her hand and she was saying, *You'll take care of him—you'll take care of him when I'm gone.* The bacon was shriveled to nothing, smoldering in the pan. I took it off the burner and served them each eight pieces, dumped the grease down the sink, and rinsed the pan with water. Steam rose up over my face, stinging my eyes. Mom eyed me. I could tell she wasn't finished. She wanted me to leave. So I walked out and started down the street, counting the street lights as they flickered on.

I went out and sat at the bottom of the lake. Weeds were starting up through the rocks. I imagined that there were fish all around me, darting all about and through me. I was breathing water. The pressure, I imagined, pushed on me in a way that made my ribs crack. I thought about Moses, how he had parted a sea. It was the soap company that'd killed the fish, but it was the sun that'd burned their home to nothing. The trees along the banks were all dead, creaky skeletons, reaching for something that seemed just out of reach. It was too late for revival, too late for resurrection, even too late for hope, and yet, in a way, it all looked so beautiful this way—it all seemed natural, just as god intended.

When I got back home, Marilynn was gone, mom was asleep in the bedroom, and Ray was out cold in the living room with the radio on and a bottle of whiskey tucked away in his fist. I went into the bathroom, unraveled the gold chain from my penis, put it in its place under the sink, and ran water over my face. I left the bible alone, kept it in the tank, and looked myself over in the mirror. There were changes taking place, I was getting older, hairs sprouting here and there, and suddenly, I felt like crying. But I didn't. I just stared at my face and wondered why time had to be such a careless monster. I wanted to stay young forever. Even more than that, I wanted Marilynn to go back to being the ten-and-a-half-year-old who let me teach her the things of the spirit, just as Joe had taught me.

From a notebook

Joe's name written across my stomach in black ink, I'm standing in front of a mirror, behind me another mirror. I'm reflected infinitely. I scratch at his name because I feel an itch. The name multiplies, spreads, and covers me. I look down at the hand I scratched with. There's a wound there, blood beginning to make a small pool in my palm—other hand, same thing. I can see a bed in the sides of my vision, but when I try to walk away from the reflection, I am suddenly paralyzed with pain and fall to the ground—feels like I've been stabbed or kicked in the liver. I lay there and watch myself die, infinitely, in the mirrors in the mirrors.

Mom died on a Saturday—pneumonia. Ray had her cremated and shoved into an urn. I didn't even cry. I couldn't. I locked myself away in my bedroom for a week. Mom didn't get a funeral. We just brought her home and put her in the kitchen, next to the radio. I stopped going to school. Ray didn't care. He turned into an even bigger mess than the mess I'd known, which was good for me, in a way. For one thing, he stopped messing with me so much. I think it was the alcohol, which was much more than the usual. He hardly ever left the couch. He didn't make breakfast anymore— day after day of no bacon, no eggs, and no orange juice. He only ever ate because I made him. I'd come home after work and make him eat gas-station sandwiches, chips, and soda. He'd nibble here and there, always reluctantly—pull away at the crust and eat a chip or two. It wasn't much, but at least it was something. It kept him alive. But even still, it didn't much help him in the long run. Pretty soon his skin started to sag off his body and his eyes sunk into the slope under his forehead. Within a few weeks he looked worse than mom looked when she died.

I held my first practice sermon within those first few weeks after mom died, in the living room, and Marilynn came over and sat on the couch with Ray. They were my two-part audience. Ray was out before I even started. But Marilynn listened to every single word, least so she said, even though, a few times, she looked more than bored. I used a lot of jerky hand gestures and read the passages from the bible I'd come to know by heart—the ones I'd given my own interpretations to. All the while, spouting scripture and giving mind, for the first time since I met her, I didn't feel the tingle, the tightening of the chain, while imagining her hands all over me, tugging and pulling and rubbing and soothing, and maybe this is why she seemed so bored, my doubts were see-thru and visible at the same time.

When I was done, I tucked Ray's legs in a blanket and told Marilynn she'd have to leave—I had something to take care of.

After she went home, I took a walk.

The walks started when the chain broke off my bike. I gave my bike to a little girl down the street, seeing no use in fixing it, but also because I'd outgrown it. There's the other thing too. I thought she was the prettiest little thing I'd ever seen. She had the tannest skin, this shortly cropped dark-brown hair, and her teeth shined brighter and whiter than any bar of soap I'd ever seen or sold. Her smile was big and looked carved, like it was made out of stone.

I stood outside her window and watched her play with her doll. She sat on the brown carpet that covered her room and let the doll walk around and drive a car and talk to a man-doll with blonde hair and muscles. I watched her for several minutes, just letting the chain tighten. There was a nice breeze that washed over my hot skin. Eventually I pulled myself out of my jeans and started the business of getting her all the way into my head. It was short lived, though, this memory making, because a dog barked, startling the poor little thing. She looked at the window, where I stood just behind the glare, and ran out of her bedroom into a hallway.

When I got home Ray was slumped over on the ground, bleeding from his head.

Jessup was the only person I knew strong enough to move a body.

I showed up at his door around eight-thirty that night, after I'd tried to move Ray alone. I could see it in his face he knew something was wrong. He had this worried look all over him.

Listen, he said. *I know you saw what happened. I'm sorry. I don't usually do things like that. I'm a good guy.*

I pushed past him, into his living room, pacing. *I don't care,* I said. *Now listen, I need your help with something.*

He looked confused but relieved, scratching his chin with a knot of fingers. *Sure,* he said, *anything. What's up?*

Tell you when we get there, I said. *You're driving.*

Jessup puked on Ray when he saw him there like that. The blood, there was so much of it. He was white as a sheet, breathing like his lungs had burst.

What the fuck, he said. *He's dead? Is he dead?*

I looked down and saw poor old Ray laying there in his own blood and nodded.

No, said Jessup. *No.*

No? I said. *What do you mean no?*

What I mean is I know I said I would help you. But I can't help with this, he said.

He paced around for a few minutes, saying *holy fuck holy fuck holy fuck.*

Holy fuck, I said, surprised at myself, those words—words I'd never said before. *What would you know about that?*

But I can't do this, he said. *For real, I just can't. It's too much.*

You said you'd do anything so long as your secret's safe with me, I said.

Why don't you just call 9-1-1? he said.

Look at him. Doesn't look like an accident. I saw it. I had a vision. I saw it. They'll try to say I had something to do with it.

Jessup bit his bottom lip, pacing like a crazy person, and then he stopped, abruptly, and put a hand up to hush me.

About a minute later, he finally said, *I'll do it, okay. I'll do it.*

We wrapped Ray in the table cloth and tied him up with some rope and phone cord. Jessup helped me clean the blood from the floor. We bleached it out. Then we picked up the apartment to give the illusion of order just in case someone barged in. I threw a bunch of clothes in my backpack, along with the rest of Ray's whiskey, my toothbrush, some toothpaste, some toilet paper, the bible, and mom. Then I helped Jessup wrangle Ray into the bed of his truck. The fake gold chain was still safe around me.

Luckily it was a short drive. When we got to the lake, Jessup backed the truck right over the rocks and got down close to where the bank used to be. We went out and found a good spot to start. We pulled up rock after rock after rock and then we started digging with our hands, making small mounds of dirt all around us.

Ray fell with a thud out of the bed of the truck. It took all the energy we could muster to pull him the hundred yards to the hole we'd dug.

The spot we'd picked was closer to the bank, a bunch of trees hanging over it, where the rocks were a bit smaller—still big but smaller—and I couldn't help but think about how I'd left parts of myself all over those rocks and now I was going to leave Ray there too.

Jessup lowered Ray into the shallow hole. It was dark but the moon was just bright enough to make out the outlines of things. Everything seemed going smoothly.

Then Jessup started this crazy stuff. He jerked his head back, like he was terrified or something, even let out a little squeal, and started pounding Ray's face with a rock the size of a large fist. I tried to stop him, but he just kept going, hitting him over and over and over again. Finally, he collapsed and let out a sigh, saying, *It moooooooved.*

What do you mean moved? I said. *He was alive?*

I don't know, man, he said. *All I know is it moved.*

You killed him, I said.

As we put the dirt and rocks over Ray, Jessup burst into tears and started blabbering about how sad it made him, having officially now killed a man. Wasn't what he thought it would be, he said.

I didn't feel it, he said. *I didn't feel powerful. I felt weak.*

I put my dirty hand on his shoulder, held it there.

I'm the lowest of the low, he said. *Scum.*

Ramirez, I said.

Jessup didn't say anything, just packed in the dirt, covered the dirt with the rocks, and then we hit the road, windows down, speeding past every stop sign.

I kept thinking Jessup was thinking what I was thinking, but he wasn't thinking anything. He shot right past 2nd Street.

I think you're forgetting something, I said.

Well fuck, he said, flipping a U-turn, and within a few minutes we pulled into her driveway.

Marilynn hopped right into the truck, not questioning a thing, just ready to go, to get away from this place, her home.

It was like she'd seen the headlights from a mile away.

We're not coming back, I said.

She nodded, as if to say *I know.*

Fucker's dead, Jessup said. *Ray's dead.*

We drove on in silence, Jessup at the wheel, Marilynn smashed between us, the tension so thick it was like something you could pick from the air and rub between your fingers.

We watched as our little town flew by, street lights blurring together as the miles stretched on. When we hit the county highways, the moon seemed to be the only thing alive out there and our hearts pumping something like rust. By the time we got onto the freeway, Marilynn was asleep, her head on my shoulder, the radio humming a low tune of country music, and Jessup, he was still all white knuckles, no mouth, and eyes on the road.

From a notebook

There's a man in a suit standing alone in a desert. The sun is scorching hot, the ground so hard you couldn't get water into it without a thousand-yard drill bit. The man is about forty, forty-five, and he's just standing there, staring into the sun. There's a small lizard perched on his shoe. He doesn't notice. He just keeps a strong gaze, searching for the soul in that ball of heat. There are no signs of sweat to be found anywhere—not on his suit, his hair, not even one little stream starting a trickle down his face. He's already been out there six hours, and he has six and six to go.

We drove and drove and drove until an even smaller town than our own town drew us in under a wash of lights. It was the kind of place we'd just left. Wasn't a soul awake in that town, not unless the window peepers were lurking in the shadows, the alcoholics and drug folks most definitely hidden away in homes, yelling, smoking, fondling unwanted children in the toxic glow of TV-light.

We holed up in the bed of the truck and one by one by one fell asleep with the stars in our eyes. I was last out. I stayed awake until the other two conked, keeping vigil over Marilynn.

In the morning, at the town's gas station, a man stood beside the trashcan smoking a cigarette and looking into the nothing of the town. People walked right past him and he didn't seem to notice them.

I took some wadded up gum wrapper from the pocket of my jeans and walked over to the trashcan. I dropped it on the ground, biding time, and lingered in a crouch a few seconds picking it up to hear what he was saying. And it sounded like he was saying some kind of prayer or something, if that's what you'd call it.

He just kept going:
Holy are you, holy are we, holy was I and am I and forever we'll be.
Holy are you, holy are we, holy was I and am I and forever we'll be.
Holy are you, holy are we, holy was I and am I and forever we'll be.

I liked the way he kept saying it, like a weird song, without altering his tone or bumping his rhythm. It was all rapid-fire, a gush of water, the way the words spilled out his mouth, little droplets of holy each and every one. Even the breaths, the spaces between the words, were something to behold. He was dirty. Little patches of dirt on his face. I could smell the smell of him, but so what, he was like a light in the dark to me. Nobody cared about the man. They didn't even seem to notice him, just as he didn't even give a nod. They all just passed by like he was nothing more than a sniff in the wind.

Then this other guy came out and said, *Come on, now, uncle Kirby. You've been out here long enough. I need you to help me with the soda order.* The man grabbed his uncle buy the elbow and led him toward the door. But he'd noticed me staring at him, too, so he stopped and said: *Sorry about my uncle. Hope he didn't bother you none. He ain't got his faculties about him anymore.*

I shrugged. *Nah, no bother.*

He nodded and started inside.

Actually, I said, *I kind of like the guy.*

The man smiled with a nod, leading his uncle Kirby through the door to do his work in the in-doors where folks wouldn't hear him speaking his truths to the wind.

I kept thinking about the old man as we drove. I felt like I'd seen him before. He had this emptiness about him. The kind of emptiness that's fuller than full.

BEGINNING
OF
ENDING

Few hours later we found ourselves in desert country. I had a sense Jessup knew where he was taking us, though I hadn't thought to ask. *Away,* was all I could think, *Away from where we'd come.*

Away from where we'll go.

We drove until sunset, when we pulled off into a little piece of land with a small house on it. The house looked pretty old. The paint was peeling off the sides and the wood was splintering.

We knocked and knocked on the front door. We waited awhile. A light was on, we could see it through one of the windows, and so we knocked again and again and again. Knocked so many times, I figured the place must be empty.

Jessup said, *She's really old—might take her a minute to get to the door.*

I nodded.

Maybe she's dead, said Marilynn.

She isn't dead, Jessup said, and then we heard some floor-creaks and shuffling. *See,* he said, *alive and kicking and about to let us in.*

The door opened slowly and there she was. Ancient face all wrinkles and big glasses that looked like something from the past. You could see all her veins through her skin when the light touched her in certain ways. She had this big black dress on and ugly pantyhose and regular brown loafers on her feet and a big gold neckless round her neck holding a crucifix against her longish boobs.

Jessup, she said. *What a surprise! Come in come in,* voice a warble of tones, crackling, but warm through and through.

We went inside and settled around in the living room. The lights were low, dim, casting shadows all against the walls and floor and ceiling. Religious pictures and statuettes and slogans were everywhere you looked. Jesus was everywhere—tacked to crosses and kneeling before subjects and floating in clouds.

We chatted a while, told a bunch of lies, made it known we'd need to stay as long as we could, as long as she'd allow us.

Stay, she said. *You can stay as long as you'd like. Only one rule if you stay, though—church isn't an option. We go at seven o'clock, every Sunday morning—and we all go together.*

Her name was Peggy and she was seventy-four years old and her home smelled like potpourri and antacid.

Strangely, never felt it for an oldie before, there was something in that face of hers, all those wrinkles and hairs and long-life, something that made the chain tighten and made my face flush, made me make up my mind to get up and find my way to the bathroom.

God, her face was wonderful, circled by a crop of short curly hair. I felt it down there, old lips, as I tugged on my penis, and it was amazing, this feeling, a revelation, and I suddenly felt I wanted this feeling forever and always beside me, with me, to touch me, to make me believe that all I'd known and done and believed was true and special and beautiful, not bad, not ugly, but pure, all of it, pure and pretty and everything we should want as humans loving humans best humans can—you could read it all in her smile, a smile filled with god and gold teeth, that things were looking up.

I wiped my hand on the floor, flushed the toilet, ran some water over my face, but, when I went back out there, I found the living room empty, a couple dim lights burning holes through the darkness.

I found them on the porch outside, drinking iced tea and talking about the constellations, speculating on the universe, just plain talking a talk without any real meaning to speak of.

I sat on a little rusty chair between Peggy and Marilynn, studied Jessup's face in the starlight. Looked like he had tears in his eyes, silent tears but tears just the same, even though he kept on in conversation like nothing was amiss and it all was lovely and mattered and we could just go on prattling on like this and be okay with the things we keep inside.

I didn't offer much in the way of conversation, just more or less listened.

Orion, right there, said Mare. *See him?*

Oh, yes, I see him all right, Peggy said.

See his belt, Mare said. *What's that dangling from his belt?* She giggled.

Young lady, Peggy said, *I don't like that kind of innuendo in my presence, you hear?*

Mare shook her head that she understood, all right, but the smirk was still firm on her face and not looking to leave.

It's a sword, said Jessup.

Yes, a sword, Peggy said. *To slay the sinners.*

A sword, said Mare. She grinned real wide. *That's a big sword.*

Peggy gave her a sharp look, Mare looked down, watched her feet shuffle nervous beneath her.

Miracles of god are nothing to joke about, are they?

No, ma'am, said Mare.

Peggy doesn't like the way you talk, said Jessup. *Apologize to her. She's nice enough to give us shelter and food and take us to church. Cut it out and apologize.*

We all sat there in a wash of awkwardness, heavy silence, sucking the cool air in.

Sorry, ma'am.

Oh, child, that's okay, it really is, Peggy said. *Just a bit of the devil in you still yet. But don't you worry—we'll get him right on out of you, yet, won't we?*

From a notebook

There's you and me and everybody who ever lived all crammed into a room. And the room, it's on fire.

That Sunday we all rose early for church. There were only about sixty other people in the congregation. Peggy was the leader of the sermon, the oldest member, the founder of the church, and I thought she did a pretty good job up there, in control and looking great, all-knowing and tough as nails.

There were quite a few younger girls there. I watched the blonde one for a while, right at the beginning, then the brown-haired one toward the middle, then the other blonde. I sensed Marilynn watching me watch them, could feel her jealousy in the heat that'd unexpectedly risen in my body. Then I felt a pinch at the back of my arm.

What the heck? I whispered.

She just looked at me like I'd fare better shut-lipped, eyes ahead.

The end is coming, folks, said Peggy to the crowd. *It's coming and coming soon. You can smell it in the air. All we see on TV and hear on the radio are signs of the coming of the horsemen. Gunmen killing innocent people, war, famine, flood, fire—you name it, it's all there, right in front of us. The end will come. But, no, it is already here.*

Right then, at that very moment, I saw a calendar, it appeared to me as though in a dream, and on it there was one day marked with pen-scribbled flames—April, 19th—but it didn't have a year on it, only the month and the day and the childish fire all covered in momma's spittle and the sound of a radio cranked past ten.

Blackness filled my sight, white ovals spinning so fast soon they were circles, voices all around me came into me, hitting me like a hundred secret atrocities, and then a tugging at my arm, more annoying than anything, suddenly pulled me away from the pain and from the darkness and opened my eyes. Mare's face slowly came into view. She was beautiful and young and amazing in a different way than I'd ever known before. There was a new glow about her I couldn't quite put my finger on.

Did you hear all that? she said. *That was amazing. I just, I don't know what to say—wow. I've never heard anything like it.*

Yeah, I said. *It was something. Peggy really has a way up there.*

Marilynn smiled, nodding, a tear in her eye, but something bad started swelling up inside me.

Somehow I got Peggy all to myself after church for a few hours, told her a little bit about myself.

God speaks through me, I said. *For a while now, I've been given visions and voices. Some are things that really end up happening, too. Other times they are just voices, commands. I always obey the voices. Everything has happened exactly how it has happened because I obey the voices. I'm supposed to be here. You are supposed to be with me. We are supposed to be here, together, right up until the end.*

I thought there would be a long pause or sneer or that she'd just brush it off like mom did. Mom listened, but she didn't really listen, not like Peggy. Peggy just giggled a strange old lady laugh, blushed, and said, *I knew you were special. The moment I set eyes on you, I knew you were a special kind of boy.* She made a long reach and ran her hand through my hair as she said it.

I knew it would come down to you and I, right here, having this talk—doing god's will, I said. *I saw it all, just a few months ago, back before mom got sick.*

You, she said, *I can tell you're a spiritual warrior.*

We were in her living room, Mare and Jessup out to fetch something to eat from the grocery store, she on the chair and me on the footstool, facing each other, knees touching, and she kept pursing her lips like she was kissing the air.

I know they're coming, I said. *I'll tell you that.*

Beg your pardon?

End of days, I said. *I know it is coming.*

She smiled this smile, real wide, held it, and said, *You welcome it?*

Yeah, I said. *It's the whole point of everything, isn't it?*

You remind me of my brother, she said. *Had visions all the way up until he was in his forties, but an accident at the paper mill left him blind, and people stopped believing him.*

Kirby? I whispered.

Peggy looked startled. *What'd you say?*

Nothing—I didn't say anything.

She stared at me a while before deciding to let it go.

They believed him? I said.

Oh, yes, every one of us did. And they're all going to believe you too. She grabbed my leg above the knee. I hardened, the chain gripping its teeth into my skin. *I mean, I believe you. Do you believe me?*

I nodded.

You really believe me? she said.

I nodded.

She moved her hand up my leg, and said: *I want to show you my love.*

That night, I had a vision of mom and Ray. I was lying on the floor and their bodies were stuck to the ceiling above me. They looked like they were treading water up there, see-thru and bizarre, twirling, like they were going to twist together and become one being under this old craggy roof. When their faces blurred together, Joe's face became them, turned to bark, and burst into flames.

I could hear Jessup and Marilynn on the couch. She seemed to be welcome to what he was doing. I didn't look. I heard her giggle a couple times and decided to let it alone, even though my blood had already thickened with heat.

The TV was on some channel selling blenders. The sound was off.

I fell asleep to a lot of heavy breathing, sounded like two people drowning in a bathtub filled with Jell-O.

Peggy woke me early the next morning. Marilynn and Jessup were still asleep and the sun hadn't yet come. She fed me a hardboiled egg in the kitchen and gave me some coffee. She rubbed my shoulders from behind the chair and said something about how I'd made her happier than she's been in quite some years.

You're welcome, I said. I smiled.

You do this thing with your lips, I said.

Now, she said. *Don't be vulgar.*

Sorry, I said.

Silence pooled a moment, the smell of the coffee almost making a sound.

Thank you, she whispered, all hidden behind her green mug.

She took a sip.

No. I said, *Thank you.*

From a notebook

A grouping of twelve to fourteen year-old girls, all holding knives—there's the Indian from the picture Mare and I saw, and Mare herself, among others of all ilk and kin, sizes, heights, hair colors, eyes, and categories. I'm in the middle of the floor, strapped there, Velcro and metal. They all have sharp smiles on their faces. I'm also smiling. But mine's sagging. Then one by one they stick their knives into me. But I don't even bleed. I only smile. The more they stab me, the more I smile, the less I bleed.

Marilynn and Jessup started spending a lot of time together. They were always making up excuses to get out of the house. Take walks. Go down to the grocery store to pick up a few things. And every time they went out, we wouldn't see them for a few hours. That's what they did this day. Jessup grabbed Mare after they'd taken turns cleaning up in the bathroom, and said, *Come with me, I've got to go down to get some cigarettes.*

Marilynn kind of jerked her shoulder back, when he touched her, and said, *And why do you have to have me go with you?*

Because you owe me some good company, he said. *That's all. You're the best company I know of.*

They stood there a minute. Then she smiled a weak one and went along with it. *All right, let's go,* she said. *You got to buy me some candy though.*

Sure, he said, *anything.*

When they left, Peggy asked me what was up with them two.

I shrugged. *They're just really close, that's all.*

Now, she said, *I want to ask you a question. I know why Jessup brought Marilynn out here. I know how bad things are for her at home. But you, I know nothing about why you're here. Where're your parents? Aren't they going to worry about you?*

No worrying to be had there, I said.

Pardon, she said.

They're both dead, I said. *Died in a car crash.*

I'm sorry, she said. *So sorry I even brought it up.*

Don't be, I said. *Their time was up, that's all. It was time for them to go. That's the way the world works—god's plans, I don't make them.*

She hung her head and moved it in circles, rubbing her neck, snapped back and looked at me.

What happened last night? she asked. *About three this morning, I woke up and heard you out here talking in your sleep.*

Don't know, I said.

Who's Joe? she asked. *You kept talking about someone named Joe.*

Just a friend I used to have, I said. *Must miss him, if I'm talking about him. Sorry if I bothered you.*

No, no, don't be silly...heard it's supposed to rain this morning, she said. *The farmers'll finally stop their bellyaching about the so-called draught, so that's good.*

Her attempt at a joke failed. There were no farmers out here. All I could offer was a faked smile.

I waited for her invitation to the bedroom while I ate another egg, even though it was morning and not the time for such things.

Didn't happen, though, not this time, but I figured somebody out there must be receiving love and spirits through 'faux pro', which is what Peggy called it, so I wasn't too upset she didn't take my hand and lead me to her bedroom. Though I felt emptier without her skin, I somehow also felt less alone.

Peggy sat on her chair in front of the muted TV, doing crossword puzzles, while I read from the bible and peeled crusts of skin from my nose and flicked them on the floor.

It was in these positions we waited for Mare and Jessup to come back home. More the hours rolled, more I started to feel like a father. Not just any father, but their father, tapping my foot on the floor, waiting for a sign that they were still alive and okay and not being corrupted by the falsehoods of the very world we'd just escaped from. I was beginning to see just a bit more clearly some things they couldn't see and it had nothing to do with any visions from above, any voices, none of that, it had nothing to do with any of those old-timey words in the good green book. It was like an animal-feeling, something I couldn't find the words for, something much beyond speaking human words and feeling human feelings and being human beings. It was beyond all that. But it wasn't divine. It just was.

What are fathers for, if not this feeling I felt in me?

It takes a little time to get people to trust you. Took me only a few weeks, and not without Peggy's help, to get the congregation behind me. Eventually, one by one by one they started to believe in the mighty visions that came into me when the lights went out at night and the sleepers slept their dreams.

Jessup even started to believe me.

Did you know I was going to do what I did with Ray?

I nodded.

Well, he said. *If you knew, why didn't you try to stop me?*

Because it was god's will, I said.

So it's all just part of some plan? he said.

Yes, I said. *It's all a part of the bigger picture.*

You fucking with me?

Nah, I said. *I wouldn't do that. And no, I don't think you're going to hell.*

Hell?

All right, I know you're not going to hell, I said. *How could you? It's all just a part of a plan that's thousands of years old.*

I never said anything about going to hell. Why you even talking about hell?

Didn't have to say it, I said. *I can see it all over your face. I can tell it's been bothering you.*

Jessup fell into stillness and silence. I could hear the wind through the leaves as though they'd been mic'd and plugged into the radio speakers. The sky looked ready to rain again. Something in all this felt electrified by Jessup's stillness, his silence, almost set on fire with intensity.

You're something else, aren't you? he said.

Marilynn said she needed to talk to me. It was the week of the annual festival the congregation put on. Goats were brought in and butchered, then roasted over a pit of coals. They made a big production out of the whole thing, with a little parade and everything, eventually ending at night with a dance and a sermon under a big white tent.

It was morning and we were walking down the street talking our usual talk about nothing, dust blowing up from the dirt roads and the sky clear as the sun rose. It was the time of the year when you can hear, if you listen closely, noises a hundred miles off—convoys of cars and trucks on highways I've never even seen, never even heard of, buzzing in my ears and sending waves through my teeth.

So we were walking and everything was normal and fine and then she stopped, jerked me back by the arm, and said, *Listen, I need to tell you something.*

Shoot, I said.

Well, this ain't for me.

Go ahead. I'm not here to judge you, I said.

Well, see, I know you know what's been going on, she said. *And, well, I love Jessup. I know I'm not supposed to, I know that, but I do,*

I love him...and...and...I'm pregnant. It's his.

Thirteen years old. By the time the baby comes, she'll be fourteen. This is just the way things are, nothing wrong with it, the way the world turns, the plan as it moves.

Mom had me young, I thought. Not that young, but young nonetheless, and I turned out just fine.

You'll be a great mother, I said.

Yeah, but the baby'll be born out of wedlock, she said. *A bastard child.*

I'm probably a bastard child myself, I said.

She gave me the hard stare, made me feel unworthy of her eyes.

What? I turned out fine, I said.

You're one of my favorite people on earth, she said. *But things change. You've changed.*

I haven't changed, I said. *Not one bit.*

She closed her hands into fists and tried to tell me that she was right and I was wrong and I'd just have to somehow live with that.

Fine, I said. *I've changed. I've changed a lot. And the biggest thing I've changed, looks like to me, is you.*

I told you, she said. *This ain't easy for me.*

From a notebook

Love

Marilynn and I, we didn't talk the rest of the day, but celebrated together that night, her mom's gold chain round my penis and a tiny little baby taking shape in her belly, moon full and terrifying in its hugeness. The whole who-is-who and what-is-what about our relationship, that whole business, left my mind as soon as night came and hugged round our campfire. We passed the bottle of whiskey I had back and forth, drinking in silence, celebrating the new growth in her belly—back and forth, back and forth until we passed out there together, our bodies a tangle on the hard ground.

It was grand, the setup they had. Children out front, teenagers and adults behind, all of us, even the dogs and the cats, parading down the street. Eventually we took a turn to the right about a mile in to get to the main spot, a huge tent staked into the sunbaked clay, and that's it, we were there, the goat roast.

There were three goats spun over coals on one huge spit. They did nine goats this way over three separate fires.

Peggy told me she'd like me to go and talk with the children. Talk to them about my visions. Tell them about the truths and powers which, at the drop of a dime, could come pouring through me. She wanted me to practice on them. Get them to like me. She wanted me to know an audience—and for them to know me. She wanted me get some real practice in, because I was due to address the congregation the following Sunday, her idea, and she didn't want me up there all foolish and nervous, but to get up there and serve them with command.

I ate two huge platefuls of chewy goat meat, then made my way to a grouping of about twelve kids, boys and girls, probably between seven and ten years old, and made them get into a circle around me. But before I even got started, before I could even blurt out the first words of my spiel, I felt it, a jolt, and my jaw tensed, my muscles went slack, and I collapsed, folding under myself on the ground. A tunnel of white light shot through me and there was this voice, and it said, *Take care of the sin that starts and begins and begins and begins before all of it comes to an end. Take away the sin before it begins and begins and begins and begins and begins the beginning again, which is always the end.*

Even more people were gathered around me. I could hear their voices, could hear their heavy lungfuls in the wind. They poured water over my face. Then they poured more water over my face. I kept hearing them, *Must be heat exhaustion.*

I could hear Peggy in the distance talking to somebody who I couldn't hear listening, *I think it might have been one of those visions I told you about.*

It is pretty hot, someone said.

He's probably dehydrated, someone said.

He just needs to get inside out of the heat, another said.

Marilynn was right there, holding me by the arm. *Come on,* she said. *You need to get home. You need some rest. You look awful.*

She helped me to my feet. I could walk just fine, but I let her hold onto me like that anyway.

When we got to the house, she helped me off with my shoes and socks and laid me out into the couch, said, *Don't move one finger. I'm going to get some water.*

I waited, didn't move.

She brought the water in. *Thanks,* I said.

She didn't say anything, just frowned and started for the door.

Where're you going? I said. *You aren't going to keep me company?*

She slammed the door shut.

From a notebook

Marilynn, damn it, she shakes her head, and says, No, I'm not keeping you company. You're a big boy. I'm going back. You just stay here, relax. Take a nap.

My head fills with a hundred dead fish and crosses and the faces of all the dead loves of my life—Joe, mom, Ray, they're all there, mixing, separating, mixing, until finally they're one and the same and look like Marilynn, if she were an old lady, glasses, scarves, saggy boobs, all of it—a wavering voice pleading with me to stop before I even begin.

I'm blind and shoving her against the front door, out of nowhere, my fist searching for the small nearly living lump in her tiny belly, over and over and over, until her breath is gone and pushed from her lungs and she's a mess of tears on the floor, asking me, Why would you do that? Why would you hit your own mother?

And all I can say is, Holy are you, holy are we, holy was I and am I and forever we'll be. Holy are you, holy are we, holy was I and am I and forever we'll be. Holy are you, holy are we, holy was I and am I and forever we'll be. Holy are you, holy are we, holy was I and am I and forever we'll be. Holy are you, holy are we, holy was I and am I

and forever we'll be. Holy are you, holy are we, holy was I and am I
and forever we'll be. Holy are you, holy are we, holy was I and am I
and forever we'll be. Holy are you, holy are we, holy was I and am I
and forever we'll be. Holy are you, holy are we, holy was I and am I
and forever we'll be. Holy are you, holy are we, holy was I and am I
and forever we'll be. Holy are you, holy are we, holy was I and am I
and forever we'll be.

It was dark when I woke up. The TV was on. The news network had a story on some big fire a hundred miles off—showed pictures of men in heavy suits around a house on fire, flooding it with water, trying to save the sinners burning in the flames.

Shit's crazy, said a whisper.

I startled back into the couch.

Some people's kids, it said.

It was Jessup. He was sitting in the chair in the corner of the room.

Jeez! I didn't see you there, I said. *You scared the crap out of me.*

Man, I could just...I could just kill her, man, he said.

Already did, I said.

What'd you mean by that? he said. *I just saw her five minutes ago down at that stupid fucking goat roast.*

Still, I said. *I love her, but she's gone.*

What the fuck are you talking about?

You're going to kill her, aren't you? I said. *That, or you or her, either way, are going to kill that baby. You're not fit to be a father.*

And you are? He said.

I remained silent.

You're crazy, man, he said. *A fucking cuckoo-cuckoo!*

And you, you're a murderer! I said. *Don't forget it, you killed a man.*

You little, you, you motherfucker, he said, and he stormed out of the house, slamming the door behind him—two peas in a pod, those two—pitching a picture of Jesus an inch to the left crooked in the entryway.

I didn't really want anybody dead. That wasn't the point.

Mare and I didn't talk the next few days. But Jessup, he wouldn't stop trying to please me. He asked if I needed anything every time they went to get groceries on their little visits down the road into town. Peggy was getting me ready for my big day, prepping me. We studied the bible constantly, six to eight hours every day, and then she'd make Marilynn and Jessup watch me deliver my sermon. Word was I was going to be the youngest person in the history of the church to be allowed up there to deliver a sermon.

Couple days before the big day, the chain broke off my penis while tugging on it in the bathroom. I was in there an hour, rethinking every movement my hand had made on my good friend Joe. His mom's paisley wallpaper, all of it, his yelling at me for wiping his stuff on the floor, his begging me to think of it as a religious experience, words from the very god himself. I'd brought mom in there, in the bathroom. She was cradled in the sink, safe, while I called out to god, my father, through myself and into myself and outward from Joe. Outward and inward from Joe. Then I fell into a lull of peace I'd never known, not once even thought a possibility. That's when it happened. The chain broke. Marilynn's dead mother's chain I kept close and near and with me at all times, it broke off right at the right moment, when my muscles hardened and everything released from inside and inside me came out.

I wiped myself on Jessup's towel and read a few verses from the bible.

I didn't have to hide it there, but still, I kept it in the tank of the toilet just as I had when mom was still alive.

When I was done, I tore the cheap chain to pieces, sprinkled the links over my cereal, and choked them down with all those soggy bits of bran.

Peggy came up behind me and rubbed my shoulders, just like she had the night we taught each other our secret languages, asked me if I wanted to go over the vocabulary again, blowing hot air at my ear.

No, I said, *I think I have it.*

All right, she said. *A genuine intellectual—a man of god! The prophet!*

Here I come, I said, smiling.

Peggy laughed a whisper and patted me on the head like a seven-year-old girl.

Mom stands there in her robe. She just stands there. She's in a white robe, her skin pale and glowing, face framed in curls, and saying stuff I can't hear or understand. I say, I can't understand. What're you saying? And again, same thing, I can't hear, I don't understand, but now she's opening her robe. She's naked beneath, left boob gone and covered in scar, and she's opening her mouth wider than any largemouth bass I ever saw. She's sending me a silent scream. I can't hear it, but it's a scream nonetheless. Then she nods and nods and nods and nods, and I'm suddenly flooded with light, the same light that takes me when I reach the max on my gold-chain tugs in the bathroom with the bible when no one else is looking. When the light leaves, there's just a pile of ashes next to an empty coffee tin. I fill the tin can with mom's ashes and drink them. I cough on her cancer.

Wake up cruel world, I began. *That's right, I said cruel world. God made it cruel so that we'd be tested to the end—the end of days. It's a test for recruitment. God doesn't want you to sit there with you thumbs in your asses, wasting away your days. Because they're not yours, they're his—those days. He wants you to arise, take arms as humans with humans, and lead the revolution. The revolution, that's right. We're talking here about the revolution against evil. We are god's army, his servants, his property, and I'll be damned if that isn't the most worthy of callings. It's the only calling. It's the only thing that matters. But let me tell you, right here and now. I see things. That's right, I have visions. Not just any visions—true visions—directives from god himself and...*

I'm going to stop you right there, Peggy said. *Sounds good—you been practicing your words, which it excellent. But, I've got to be honest with you—t sounds a bit pedantic or even patronizing. You need to draw them in, you just being you. I know you will. You have that power, you have that in you. People are drawn to the kind of thing you already have: naivety, innocence, and youth. You'll be more convincing if you talk to them like you talk to me, know what I mean?*

I felt bad, you know, I'd let her down, but still, I'd been working hard to get it right, so it wasn't easy letting it go.

But those words, the ones we've been working on. Throw them in, just do it when it's least expected, you know, so you can meet them on their level, she said.

Okay, I said. I didn't get it, not fully, but I understood it, in a way, and it didn't matter anyway, because an hour later, I told her I wasn't going to give no sermon that Sunday.

But you've worked so hard, she said. *We've worked so hard on this, together.*

I know, I said. *But I just want to be a kid for a while, you know. I want to preach someday, just not right away. I know I have a gift. I know god speaks through me. Isn't that enough, for now? I just want to do things like a normal kid for once.*

I could tell I'd severely let her down, but she was cool, said, *I understand, honey. We'll get you up there when you are good and ready. But in the meantime, don't you be neglecting me, you hear.*

I shook my head. *Yes, ma'am. Why would I ever want to do that?*

Around lunchtime, Jessup wanted to talk. Said he was sorry for acting the way he'd acted after the goat roast.

It's all right, I said. *I understand. You're going through a lot right now.*

He just shook his head, staring at me, slamming a pack of smokes against his hand. Then he walked outside and got into his truck. He revved the engine a few times and sped off, throwing dirt and pebbles against the house.

Jessup didn't come home. He was gone the rest of the day, didn't come home that night, and nobody seemed to care or even worry, which was strange.

At nine Peggy went into her bedroom, giving me a signal with her eyes on the way in, and I watched as the light under her door faded and faded and then steadied to black.

Mare and I were glued in front of some stupid TV show, volume low, subtitles, when I reached over and started rubbing her belly, smiling.

I was surprised, because she didn't resist, not a bit. She just looked at me and smiled.

We looked at each other for a while, both of us happy, and then, out of nowhere she started kissing me, taking me to that place, the place we'd first kissed, in my mind.

Finally, I stood and took her hand, helped her to her feet, and started toward Peggy's room. She followed me, not questioning a thing, not even when I opened the door and told Peggy, *We have a visitor.*

Peggy's silence was an invitation.

I quietly shut the door behind us.

Searching the secrets in their wombs, the silent words of god,

I found the only possible word, the best expression of my love, in a glowing ball of heat.

I wander into the desert all alone and half-asleep, Peggy and Marilynn still snuggled up to each other in bed. I start off at sunrise and find a spot about a mile, mile-and-a-half deep, sit down on the hard clay and watch the clouds fold and form into shapes above me, the sun slowly punching itself up and up and up over the horizon, and then, like a smear over my dreaming eyes, over my entire life, a dark haze fills the air, a smell of distant smoke, and I know, I've known all along, that that old craggy house had burst into flames before I ever even left it. I shut my eyes. The sun fills me. I blink. I'm still alive.

ACKNOWLEDGEMENTS

Thank you: J David Osborne, Mathew Revert, Michael J Seidlinger, Kevin Sampsell, Jamie Iredell, Brandon Hobson, Mike Young, Nat Baldwin, Juliet Escoria, Brian Alan Ellis, Jeff Jackson, Brian Evenson, Scott McClanahan, Tim Hecker, Wu-Tang Clan, and John Fahey, for being friendly, encouraging, inspiring, and helping me to get through this.

Elizabeth, you are everything good in this world.

ABOUT THE AUTHOR

Troy James Weaver is the author of *Witchita Stories, Temporal, Selected Stories,* and *Marigold.* His stories have been published widely online and in print. He lives in Wichita, Kansas with his wife and dogs.

Printed in Great Britain
by Amazon

43970886R00078